For the young
of all ages
at Christmas
everywhere

Margaret K. McElderry Books
An imprint of Simon & Schuster Children's Publishing Division
1230 Avenue of the Americas, New York, New York 10020
Copyright © 2003 by Demi

The text for this book is set in Packard.
The illustrations for this book are rendered in paint and ink.
Manufactured in China
1 2 3 4 5 6 7 8 9 10
Library of Congress Cataloging-in-Publication Data
Demi.
The legend of Saint Nicholas / Demi. — 1st ed.
p. cm.
Summary: Recounts pivotal events in the history and life of Saint Nicholas,
including how he came to be associated with Christmas and Santa Claus.
ISBN 0-689-84681-9
1. Nicholas, Saint, Bp. of Myra — Juvenile literature. [1. Nicholas, Saint, Bp. of Myra.
2. Saints. 3. Santa Claus.] I. Title. BR1720.N46 D46 2003
270.2'092 — dc21
2002008426

FIRST
EDITION

THE LEGEND OF SAINT NÍCholas

Demí

Margaret K. McElderry Books

NEW YORK   LONDON   TORONTO   SYDNEY   SINGAPORE

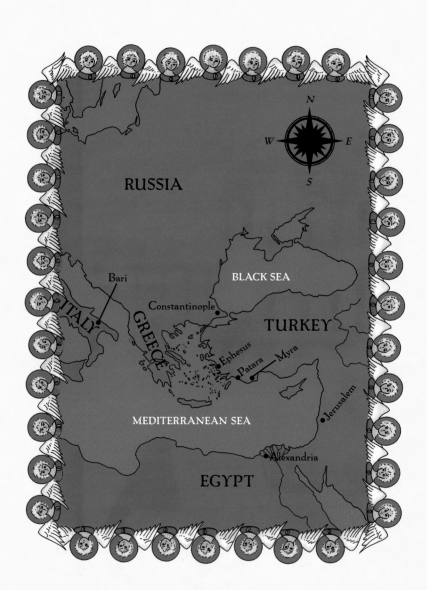

Nicholas was born to noble Christian parents, Johanna and Epiphanes, in around the year A.D. 280 in Patara, Lycia, in Asia Minor, which is now Turkey.

As soon as he was born, Nicholas showed amazing and miraculous powers. On his very first day he stood up in his bath and prayed to God!

As a toddler, Nicholas
fasted on every holy saint's day.
He refused to nurse,
preferring to pray all day.

And as a young boy, Nicholas preferred attending church to playing with other children. He loved to sing hymns and recite the Holy Scriptures, all of which he knew by heart.

Nicholas was a sensitive child, deeply saddened by the sickness, suffering, old age, and death that he witnessed every day. He vowed to always help everyone everywhere in any way he could.

When his parents died in a plague, Nicholas inherited great wealth. He made it his purpose in life to use all of his wealth and strength to help people in need and to glorify the Lord.

There lived in Lycia a fine nobleman with three daughters who had fallen on hard times. The man was desperate, unable to provide dowries for his daughters, and he felt he had no choice but to sell them to prospective husbands.

Young Nicholas learned of the man's misfortune, and late one night, he knotted a pile of coins into a cloth and went to the nobleman's house.

Nicholas soundlessly tossed the sack in through an open window. The next morning, the nobleman found the coins and wept for joy, praising God. He would not have to sell his oldest daughter. But he would still have to sell the other two.

That night, Nicholas again tossed a sack of coins through the nobleman's window. And on the third night he came back with a third sack of coins. This time, the sack of coins landed in the youngest girl's stocking. The nobleman was awakened, and he pursued Nicholas, crying, "Stop! Stop! Please let me meet you. Let me thank you!"

The nobleman caught up with Nicholas, falling to the ground and kissing his feet. The humble Nicholas asked that the nobleman never reveal his identity until after his death.

Some people say it was this act of Nicholas's anonymous generosity that resulted in the Christmas tradition of St. Nicholas (or Santa Claus) leaving gifts for children in stockings or shoes.

Nicholas continued to help the poor and the needy near his home. Then he decided to travel to further his knowledge and broaden his understanding of people and places.

He made a pilgrimage to the holy land of Jerusalem. On the way he recited the Beatitudes of Christ:

"Blessed are the poor in spirit,
for theirs is the kingdom of Heaven.
Blessed are those who mourn,
for they will be comforted.
Blessed are the meek,
for they will inherit the earth.
Blessed are those who hunger
and thirst for righteousness,
for they will be filled.
Blessed are the merciful,
for they will receive mercy.
Blessed are the pure in heart,
for they will see God.
Blessed are the peacemakers, for they
will be called the children of God.
Blessed are those who are persecuted
for righteousness' sake, for theirs is
the kingdom of Heaven."

Nicholas traveled as far
as Alexandria, Egypt, a great
center of learning.

In the coastal town of Myra, near Patara, the priests were choosing a new bishop. Early one morning, one of the priests heard an inner voice telling him to wait at the church doors and make bishop the first person to come by, whose name would be Nicholas.

Nicholas, just returning from his travels home to Patara, approached the church in Myra.

"What is your name, young man?" asked the priest.

"Nicholas, the servant of Your Holiness," Nicholas replied.

At that, all the priests of Myra fell to their knees and rejoiced in their new bishop.

Nicholas brought to his new position a sense of deep piety, humility, and great enthusiasm. He remains to this day the youngest man ever to be made a bishop.

Not everyone during this time was a believer in Jesus Christ, and in around the year 305, when Emperor Diocletian was in power in Asia Minor, Nicholas suffered greatly during a persecution of the Christians. Under torture, Nicholas supposedly defended his faith in God and Jesus Christ in a glorious confession. For this, he was given the name "The Confessor."

In the year 325, during the reign of Emperor Constantine I, it is thought that Nicholas was again tormented for his beliefs and put on trial during the first ecumenical Council of Nicaea. The emperor was about to rule against Nicholas when suddenly an image of Christ and the Mother of God appeared in the sky over Nicholas. This holy apparition so impressed the emperor that Nicholas was saved, his bishopric preserved.

News of this and other miracles surrounding Nicholas spread far and wide. People from Scythia, India, Africa, Italy, and the farthest corners of the world traveled to Asia Minor to see, touch, and hear the great Bishop Nicholas of Myra.

One night,
there was a
violent storm at sea
near the coast of Lycia.
Sailors caught in the storm were
praying for their lives and cried
out for Nicholas to help them.

Immediately, an apparition
appeared in the sky saying, "You
cried out to me and here I am!"
The apparition commanded the
waves to be calm, and the sailors
were saved.

A short
time later,
the sailors passed
by a church where
Nicholas was preaching.
They recognized Nicholas as
the man whose apparition had
saved them from death, and
they fell down in prayer.

From then on, Nicholas
became the patron and
protector of seafarers and
anyone who worked on the sea.

A time came when Myra suffered a great famine and people were starving to death. A wicked innkeeper kidnapped three little boys, killed them, and salted them in a tub of brine, intending to serve them as food.

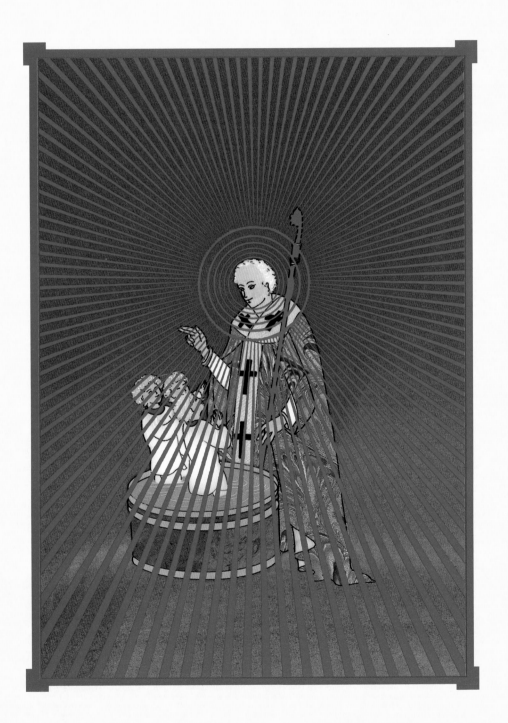

But Nicholas, who loved children, learned of the evil deed and imprisoned the innkeeper. Then, praying to his Lord, Nicholas raised the boys' bodies from the brine and restored them to life.

From then on, Nicholas became the patron and protector of children.

Another story about Nicholas tells of a young boy named Dmitri who was swimming and drowned in the Dnieper River in what is now Russia. He was pronounced dead, and his family prepared to mourn their great loss. But the next morning, Dmitri was found alive and well, sitting and playing on the steps of Nicholas's cathedral in Myra. There was no doubt in the minds of many that Nicholas had saved the child.

Time and again, Nicholas protected children from harm and saved them from death, appearing miraculously to punish the wicked and free the innocent.

Nicholas once appeared in a dream to Emperor Constantine, telling him to release three men from prison who had been wrongfully accused of a crime. So vivid was the dream that, upon waking, the emperor released the men.

And from then on, Nicholas became the patron and protector of prisoners and captives.

In early December of the year 342 or 343, Nicholas felt his spirit being drawn strongly to Heaven. He knew his earthly body would soon die, and he prayed to God to send angels to bring him home.

Suddenly, angels appeared to Nicholas. He cried, "Into your hand, O Lord, I commend my spirit!" and he rose to Heaven.

His body was buried in a shrine in Myra, where, some people believed, his bones exuded a fragrant healing oil. Reports of his miracles steadily increased.

It is said that Nicholas performed no less then twenty miracles during his lifetime. He was sainted after his death, and later, Emperor Justinian I built the great Church of St. Nicholas in Constantinople, which is now Istanbul, Turkey.

For many years St. Nicholas's shrine in Myra was the center of pilgrimage, until the year 1087, when Italian merchants removed the saint's earthly remains and reburied them in Bari, Italy. The Church of St. Nicola was built in Bari soon thereafter.

The miracles of St. Nicholas and the cult of Nicholas became more popular throughout the Western world. Because of his reputation as a patron of seafarers, he became the patron saint of seafaring places, such as Greece, Sicily, Holland, and the river towns of Germany.

Over time St. Nicholas became the patron saint not only of seafarers, children, and prisoners, but also of pilgrims, travelers, voyagers, maidens, choirboys, firefighters, stonemasons, weavers, and butchers.

In the centuries after his body passed into Heaven, St. Nicholas remained one of the most popular saints. During the Middle Ages in Europe, his feast day, celebrated on December 6, was a time of great merriment and gift giving.

Because of St. Nicholas's reputation as a lover and protector of children, a young boy was chosen to play the part of St. Nicholas during his feast day celebration. The boy saint led a grand procession into a church, amid trumpets, organ music, songs, and prayers.

In Germany, Sweden, Switzerland, and the Netherlands the custom arose of giving gifts in St. Nicholas's name during the Christmas season.

In Holland in the Middle Ages, Dutch children grew up with a festive custom of leaving hay and sugar in their shoes on the eve of St. Nicholas's feast day. St. Nicholas—or Sinter Klaas, as he is known there—gave the hay and sugar to his horse, and in turn, filled the children's shoes with nuts and candies.

Dutch Protestants brought their traditional beliefs in the gift-giving Sinter Klaas with them when they founded New Amsterdam, now New York. They popularized the belief in the generous, child-loving figure throughout America.

Because St. Nicholas's feast day is in December, so close to when Christmas is celebrated, over time the figure of Sinter Klaas soon was transfigured into the character we call "Santa Claus."

Throughout the world today, whether he goes by the name of St. Nicholas, Sinter Klaas, or Santa Claus, this figure who shows enormous generosity, a love of children, deep care for the poor and needy, and a completely selfless nature is considered to embody the spirit of Christmas and the true spirit of the Lord.

THE PRAYER OF ST. NICHOLAS

*We call upon
Your mercy, O Lord.
Through the intercession
of St. Nicholas,
keep us safe amid all dangers
so that we may go forward
without hindrance
on the road to salvation.*